D1289847

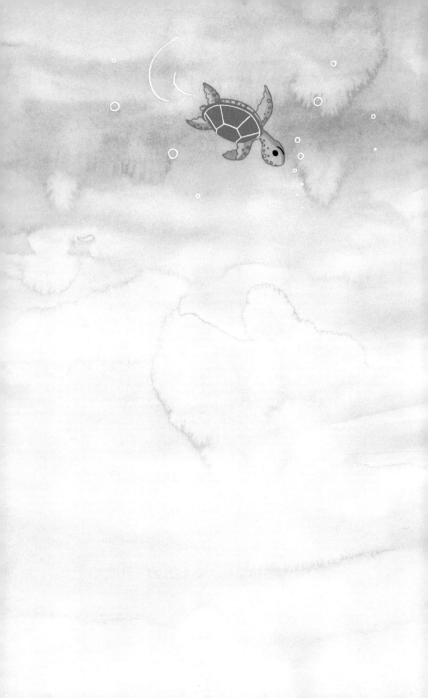

Five reasons why you'll love Emerald...

Dive into a magical underwater kingdom!

Emerald's best friend is a little octopus called Inkibelle.

Emerald is learning about being a mermaid princess—but she's doing it *her* way.

Gorgeous green and black pictures.

Emerald's friends are the best a mermaid could wish for. Meet Oceana, Finn, Marina and Aqua.

Emerald's underwater pet is an octopus called Inkibelle. What would your dream underwater pet be?

A pet pufferfish
called Spike-Stella.—
Elin

A dolphin.
I love the way they
jump in the sea.—
Esme

A glittery shark
called Sparky.—
Jennifer

I'd play games with a pet
seal, and we'd do roly-polies
together in the water!—
Zazie

A jellyfish, and we'd
eat raspberry jelly all
day. — Skyla

A crab.
I would call him
Fweetoo. — Bertie

I'd go for rides on
my pet squid. —
Sam

An electric eel and a stingray.
I would get electricity from the eel. —
Felix

A sea dragon who
could blow bubbles. —
Amna

A stingray because
they are cool. —
Jace

Scallop City

Town Hall

Marina's House →

Finn's House

Park

Palace

Princess Delphina's School

eana's
House

← Emerald's
Dad's House

Emerald's School ←

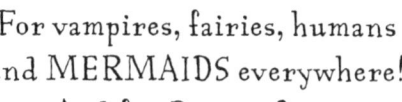
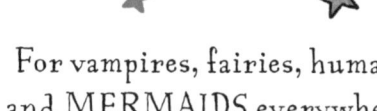

For vampires, fairies, humans
and MERMAIDS everywhere!
And for Bonnie Ocèa.

OXFORD
UNIVERSITY PRESS

Great Clarendon Street, Oxford OX2 6DP

Oxford University Press is a department of the University of Oxford.
It furthers the University's objective of excellence in research, scholarship,
and education by publishing worldwide. Oxford is a registered trade mark
of Oxford University Press in the UK and in certain other countries

Database right Oxford University Press (maker)

First published in 2023

British Library Cataloguing in Publication Data

Data available

ISBN:978-0-19-278397-4

1 3 5 7 9 10 8 6 4 2

Printed in Great Britain by Bell and Bain Ltd, Glasgow

Paper used in the production of this book is a natural,
recyclable product made from wood grown in sustainable forests.
The manufacturing process conforms to the environmental
regulations of the country of origin.

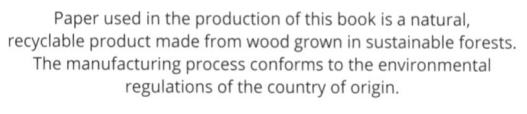

EMERALD

and the Ocean Parade

Harriet Muncaster

OXFORD
UNIVERSITY PRESS

Chapter ONE

TRRRRINGGGG went my clamshell alarm clock.

I sat up in bed feeling confused for a moment before I remembered where I was—in my bedroom in the royal palace! A few months ago, my mum and King Auster

got married, which I suppose makes *me* a princess. I have two houses because I spend half my time at the palace and half with my dad who lives in a small pearly pink house on the other side of Scallop City. I was still getting used to living in two different places and I was still getting used to being a princess. I didn't feel like one at all yet. I don't look anything like my graceful stepsister Delphina. My hair is all spiky and wild (which is exactly how I like it) and I have a wriggly little octopus for a pet!

I slipped out of bed, uncurling my tail. Tiny bubbles danced in the water.

'Come on Inkibelle!' I said to my pet

octopus who was still snoozing soundly on my sea-sponge pillow. 'Time to get up for school!'

Inkibelle does not like getting up for school.

I poked her but she only curled up tighter so I left her snoozing while I swam out of my bedroom and down the shell-studded corridor to the bathroom. On my way, I bumped into Delphina.

'Emerald,' she cried. 'Good morning!' Then she stretched her arms out wide and I knew she was coming in for a hug. Delphina is a very affectionate mermaid. I found her a tiny bit annoying when I first moved in to the palace a few months ago, but

I am getting used to her now.

'I'll race you to breakfast!' she cried, and then swished away in a flurry of bubbles.

'You're late!' said Mum when I finally made it down to the grand dining room, with Inkibelle swimming along behind me.

'Sorry!' I said. 'Inkibelle just didn't want to get up this morning!'

Inkibelle poked me crossly with one of her tentacles and pouted.

'Well it's *true*!' I said as I sat down next to Delphina, who was already tucking in to some sea-crunch cereal.

I pulled a slice of mermaid toast towards me and spread it thickly with pale green seaweed butter.

'We've been talking about the Ocean Parade!' said Delphina excitedly. 'I can't wait!'

Immediately I felt my insides fizz with excitement. I *love* the Ocean Parade! It happens every year to celebrate the new summer sea season arriving and I've been to it since I was a tiny mermaid. There's lots of delicious food, music and dancing, and everyone dresses up. Dressing up is my favourite part! A stream of pretty floats parade through the streets of Scallop City, including the royal carriage.

Last year I went to the parade with my
school friends and it was the best day ever!
We dressed up in all our spangles and
sparkles, ate crispy-kelp and sea-flower
floss and danced to music as the floats
paraded by. I smiled as I remembered all
the fun we'd had.

'I can't wait either!' I said.

Delphina grinned happily
at me. 'What kind of
headdress will you wear
Emerald?'

'Well, last year me
and my friends bought
sea-flower crowns from
a stall and . . .'

'I mean which *royal* headdress will you choose!' said Delphina. 'You'll be in the carriage with the royal family this year remember! It's tradition for us all to wear big fancy headdresses!'

I frowned and looked at Mum and Auster but they both just smiled and nodded.

'Your first parade in the royal carriage!' said Mum. 'Won't that be exciting!'

'Um . . .' I said. It hadn't occurred to me that I would have to ride in the royal carriage during the parade, but I supposed that I would have to, now I was a mermaid *princess*.

It was taking some getting used to.

'But the royal carriage rides through the centre of Scallop City and then ends up back at the palace,' I said. 'We won't have time to join in any of the fun!'

'There will be a special party back here at the palace,' smiled Auster. 'With very fancy food!'

I thought back to the crispy-kelp and sea-flower floss I had bought from a stall last year. I doubted there would be anything like that served at the palace. I don't think I'm really cut out to be a *proper* princess, I thought despondently.

I didn't look like one.

I didn't *eat* like one.

And I definitely didn't *feel* like one!

'Do I *have* to go in the royal carriage?' I asked. 'I'd much rather hang out with my school friends.'

Delphina's face fell and Auster looked a bit disappointed.

'I *mean*,' I said hurriedly. 'I don't think anyone will want to see *me* in the carriage,'

'Of course they will!' said Auster. 'You're a mermaid princess now! You absolutely have to be there.'

'You do,' agreed Mum firmly.

I sighed, putting my piece of toast back onto my plate. Suddenly I didn't really feel very hungry. The thought of not being able to go to the Ocean Parade with my friends was not a nice feeling. And the thought of having to sit in the royal carriage and be on show to everyone in the kingdom was even worse! I was nothing like Delphina. She looks and acts like a proper princess. I'm just . . . *me.*

'There's a headdress fitting this afternoon after school,' said Auster. 'It'll be fun, I promise.'

I nodded glumly and Mum tried to reassure me with an encouraging glance.

'Don't worry Emerald,' she said.

'We'll find a headdress you really like.'

I gave her a watery smile.

'Maybe,' I said doubtfully.

15

Chapter TWO

Delphina and I left the palace and swam to school, with Inkibelle swishing along behind us. Delphina doesn't have a special pet but she does have a magical merteddy bear! (A vampire-fairy called Isadora Moon magicked it alive for her when she was visiting our underwater kingdom!) Delphina's merteddy goes everywhere

with her, just like Inkibelle comes
everywhere with me!

We reached Mrs Shell-Clackers
Academy for Young Merpeople and
Delphina waved goodbye. We go to different
schools and she has to swim a little further.

I swam into the playground and spotted my friends right away. Marina, Oceana, Finn, and Aqua were huddled over a notebook, looking very busy with something.

'Hi Emerald!' said Marina, looking up. 'We're just designing our outfits for the Ocean Parade. Look, here's mine!'

She held the notebook out towards me and I stared at the page, impressed.

Marina had designed a beautiful top with swathes of floaty material that would swirl behind her in the water. She was going to wear lots of pearl necklaces and stick pearl beads all the way up and down her arms too.

'Oh!' I breathed. 'It's so *you!*'

'That's what I said!' Oceana smiled.

I couldn't help but feel a tiny bit jealous. I wished I could wear exactly what I wanted to the Ocean Parade. But unlike my friends, I was going to have to wear a stupid old headdress and sit in the royal carriage!

'Hey, let's design your outfit Emerald!' said Oceana. 'I expect you'll want something a bit more edgy with lots of sparkly dark greens in it.'

'I *would*,' I said. 'Except I'm sure I won't be allowed to dress how I usually do. I have to sit in the royal carriage this year wear a special royal headdress!'

'Really?' Marina sounded excited and a little bit disappointed, all at once.

'I thought you were coming to the parade with us,' said Finn.

'I thought I was,' I huffed.

'Don't you want to sit in the royal carriage?' asked Aqua. 'I think it sounds like fun.'

'I doubt it,' I said miserably. 'I'll probably do something un-princess-like and everyone will laugh.'

'You really *are* the most unlikely mermaid to become a princess!' Marina smiled.

I felt a bolt of worry zing through me.

'*That* is what I'm worried about!' I replied. 'I don't feel like a princess at all?!'

Marina put her arm around me.

'Don't worry Emerald, you'll be great! And we'll all make sure to wave at you as you go past!'

'We'll feel *proud* to see our friend in the royal carriage!' added Aqua.

'Thanks,' I replied, blushing and hiding my face under my spiky mop of black hair. My friends always know what to say to make me feel better.

24

At the end of the day, Oceana asked if I wanted to go over to her house.

'The others are coming too,' she said. 'We're going to play catch the bubble!'

'Count me in,' I replied.

Catch the bubble is a special merpeople game where you have to race each other through the water after a silvery, magic bubble. It's very tricksy! The first one to catch the bubble is the winner. I felt excited as I packed away my things and swung my schoolbag over my shoulder, following Oceana, Marina, Finn, and Aqua into the playground. When I got outside, I was surprised to find my mum waiting for me. She never usually comes to pick me up from school.

'What are you doing here?' I asked.

'Don't you remember?' she said. 'We've got our headdress fitting.'

'Do I *have* to go?' I asked. 'I *really* want to go over to Oceana's and play catch the bubble!'

'Yes, Emerald, you do,' replied Mum. 'It's all booked in at Madame Cowrie's!'

'Oh,' I said again. I looked at my friends and shrugged.

'We can play catch the bubble another time,' said Marina.

'We'll see you tomorrow Emerald!' said Finn.

I watched wistfully as my friends swam away together, chatting and laughing.

Without *me*.

It wasn't busy at Madame Cowrie's shop that afternoon because the whole place had been cordoned off especially for our visit.

We swam through the doors, into the posh boutique.

'Emeraaald!' squealed Delphina excitedly. 'I can't wait for our fitting. Aren't you excited?'

'Erm,' I said, not wanting to hurt her feelings. 'I suppose so.'

Delphina, Mum, and I swam over to where Auster was trying on headdresses. They were all very regal looking.

'The bigger the better I say!' he declared placing a very large, very ornate looking headdress on top of his head. It was dripping with gold coins and gems that tinkled when he moved.

'What do you think?' he asked, turning towards us. Delphina clasped her hands together, grinning.

'I love it Dad! I want one just as big and fancy!'

★ ★ ★

I watched as Mum and Delphina had fun trying on lots of different styles. There were so many to choose from—twirly and swirly, ritzy and pearly. They all looked very . . . *royal*. And totally not *me*.

I hugged Inkibelle close and I think I must have hugged her a tiny bit too hard because she suddenly shot out of my arms in a flurry of bubbles, catapulting up onto the shelves above my head.

'Watch out!' Delphina shouted, as a
large headdress fell down from the shelf
above, and landed right on my head!
Inkibelle must have knocked it off!

'Ow!' I cried. I tried to pull the crown
off but the fiddly little jewels kept tangling

in my wavy spiky hair. I pulled harder but it seemed to just make everything worse. Every time I managed to get one part of the crown free, another part got stuck!

'Oh dear, let me help!' said Madame Cowrie, swimming towards me with a large pair of shiny silver scissors.

I stared at her in horror.

'You can't cut my hair!' I gasped.

'I'm afraid I'll have to snip a *few* little bits off,' replied Madame Cowrie. 'But don't worry. I'll only cut what's absolutely *necessary*. No one will notice with your hairstyle under the headdress anyway!'

Suddenly, I was surrounded by Mum, Auster, and Delphina, all watching Madame Cowrie snip, snip with her scissors. I felt my cheeks blush and eventually the headdress was free.

'There!' said Mum. 'No one will even notice your hair!'

I swam towards the centre of the room, keeping well away from the shelves. I could see Inkibelle hiding behind one of the headdresses with a guilty expression on her face.

'Can we get on with choosing our headdresses now?' said Delphina.

'Yes!' said Mum excitedly, as she placed an extremely pretty and delicate crown upon her head. 'Which one will you choose Emerald?'

I looked around Madame Cowrie's shop. Pearls, jewels, and sea-glass winked down at me from every shelf, but I just couldn't imagine myself wearing any of it.

'I don't think there's anything really in my style,' I said.

'Oh of course there is!' replied Mum, swiftly.

'Look at *meee!*' shouted Delphina as she whirled round the shop, wearing the biggest, most majestic headdress she could find. Auster took her hands and they spun

together in the water, little bubbles twirling

up towards the octopus-shaped chandelier.

I watched them dance, feeling like there

was a wriggly octopus inside *me*.

'Do you need some help Emerald?' asked Auster, swimming over with Delphina.

'How about this one?' she asked, picking up a large silver headdress with stars all over it. It still didn't feel as though it was quite me but I had to admit that it was pretty. And I could tell that Delphina was trying to be helpful.

'That one will be fine,' I said, pasting a smile onto my face. 'Thank you Delphina.'

Chapter THREE

The following evening, we had a rehearsal for the Ocean Parade. The royal carriage pulled up outside the palace and we all swam out to admire it. It was very beautiful—round like a giant silver bubble, and decorated all over with swirls, twirls, and jewels. Six beautiful dolphins were harnessed to the front of the carriage, looking very regal.

'I love dolphins!' exclaimed Delphina, putting out her hand to pat on of them on the snout. The dolphin squeaked happily.

'Right!' said Auster. 'Everyone get inside the carriage! The dolphins will pull it around the palace gardens and we will practise our waving technique. The Ocean Parade is only two days away!'

He swam into the carriage and sat down on one of the squashy sea-sponge seats. Mum and Delphina followed with me at the back, and Inkibelle squiggling along behind me. I sat down on the seat next to one of the large, open windows.

There was nowhere to hide—*everyone* would be able to see in as we passed!

'Be careful Emerald!' said Mum, as I accidentally knocked my headdress into her delicate one. A single pearl came floating off her headdress, and landed in her lap.

'Oops, sorry,' I said.

'No worries Emerald, I'm sure it can be mended before the parade.' Mum smiled at me but I felt bad. I knew how excited Mum was about the headdress she had chosen.

There was a sudden jerk and the carriage started to float through the palace gardens, pulled along by the dolphins. We passed tall seaweed fronds in all the colours of the rainbow. Colourful fish darted about alongside the carriage. They were pretty to look at but I couldn't help remembering that the day after tomorrow it wouldn't be just fish that I would be seeing outside the carriage window. It would be faces. Hundreds and hundreds of them! Staring at me, wearing my big silver *princessy* headdress.

'We wave like this,' said Auster,
showing me how to swish my hands
through the water in a regal way.

'And we smile,' he added. 'Don't forget to smile!'

Mum and Delphina waved and smiled, beaming out of the carriage windows at the fish. I tried to do the same.

'Maybe a little more enthusiastically,

Emerald,' said Auster,
kindly.

I waved my
hand faster and harder,
accidentally bopping
Inkibelle so that she swooshed through
the water, leaving a dark ink cloud
behind her that sank down into the
sea-sponge seats.

'Maybe just wave a little bit slower,'
coached Mum, sounding a little worried
as she glanced at the ink-stained seat.
'And perhaps you should leave Inkibelle at
home for the parade?'

'No!' I gasped.

I stopped waving for a moment,

feeling my heart beating hard in my chest. I was starting to feel very uncomfortable indeed. Inkibelle came everywhere with me. It wouldn't be fair to leave her at home! I looked down at my hands. First I wasn't waving enough and then I was waving too much—this would never do—I would never be able to look or act like a proper princess!

'Are you all right Emerald?' asked Mum, putting her hand on my tail.

'I'm fine,' I said.

But I wasn't fine. I didn't feel very princessy at all. I imagined merpeople lining the parade and saying, *What in the name of glimmering gills is that mermaid doing in the royal carriage!'*

'I have to go to the bathroom,' I said, but then I scooted out of the carriage so fast that my tail got caught in the door.

'OUCH!' I yelled. I tugged my tail
free and tumbled over into a huge clump
of seaweed nearby. The giant, slimy
fronds waved about, encircling me.
It felt like being wrapped up by a squid!

52

A big, cold, slimy squid!

'Halt the carriage!' yelled Auster.

I looked up and saw Mum, Auster, and Delphina staring down at me from the carriage window.

'Let me help you!' said Auster, opening the carriage door.

'No!' I shouted, hurriedly unpeeling the seaweed fronds from where they were curled around my body. I just wanted to be alone, in a place where I could just be myself and not make any more mistakes.

I swam as fast as I could back into the palace and up to my room. I took off my headdress and threw it on the bed, staring crossly at it. I thought of Mum, Auster, and Delphina all looking so perfect and doing the wave properly and not falling over. I just didn't fit in!

I looked over at my little suitcase. Perhaps I should go and stay at Dad's house just until the Ocean Parade was over. He was away on holiday until next week but that was OK because I wanted to be completely *alone.*

I began to throwing things into my suitcase. Some clothes, my jewellery, my favourite black tiara, my clamshell alarm clock, and Inkibelle's bow.

I was slamming the suitcase shut when there was a knock on the door.

'Emerald?' called Auster. 'Emerald, can I come in?'

I stared at my suitcase and hurriedly shoved it under my duvet.

'Come in,' I said.

'Are you all right Emerald?' Auster asked, swimming into my room.

'Um . . .' I mumbled, looking into my lap.

'I just wanted to check that everything is OK.'

Auster tentatively sat down next to me on my bed, right on top of my suitcase. Uh-oh . . .

'Ooh!' he said, jumping up and rubbing his tail. 'Your mattress isn't very comfortable!'

He whisked my duvet off and saw my suitcase. Auster frowned, but didn't say anything. Instead, he sat back down but *next* to the suitcase this time, and looked thoughtfully around my room.

'You know,' he said. 'I was very nervous the first time I took part in the Ocean Parade. I was worried I wouldn't get the waving right. My hand felt like a wobbly jellyfish!'

I couldn't help smiling a little bit. The idea of Auster with a jellyfish for a hand was funny!

'My father gave me some good advice,' said Auster. 'He told me to just be myself! All you can do is be yourself Emerald. I'm sorry if we made you feel as though you had to act a certain way. There's absolutely no point in pretending you're someone you're not.'

I looked down at my lap and fidgeted with my hands.

'But I don't feel princessy at all!' I whispered.

'Being a princess is whatever *you* make it,' said Auster. 'You are who you are and becoming a princess shouldn't change that. I *want* you to be yourself!'

'But what if I decide I don't want to be in the parade at all?'

'It's important to me that you feel comfortable Emerald,' Auster said, 'and I certainly don't want to make you do anything you don't want to do. Maybe sleep on it and see how you feel in the morning?'

I nodded. That was fair.

'OK,' I agreed.

I felt much better after my chat with Auster. He had pretty much said that I didn't have to go in the carriage if I didn't want to, so I decided that I wouldn't!

I put my suitcase away and snuggled under the covers with Inkibelle, feeling pleased. But as I drifted off to sleep, I began to feel a little uneasy. Something was nagging at me. Was there a way to ride in the royal carriage *and* be myself at the same time?

Chapter FOUR

I woke up the next morning with a plan.
The Ocean Parade was tomorrow so I
didn't have much time!

I swooshed out of bed in a flurry
of bubbles and swam down to the great
dining hall. 'Mum!' I said excitedly. 'Please
can I go over to Oceana's house after
school today? Please, please, please!'

Mum blinked in surprise.

'Well, good morning to you too, Emerald!' she said. 'Erm, I don't know about you going to a friend's house *this* evening. It's the Ocean Parade tomorrow. Whether you're coming in the carriage with us or not, you need to be well-rested tonight.'

She smiled at me but I could see that she looked a little worried.

'Pleeeeease!' I begged. 'It's really important!'

'Well all right,' she said. 'But don't be home too late.'

As soon as I got to school, I found Oceana

and asked if I could come over to her house at the end of the day.

'Of course!' she replied. 'Shall we ask the others too? Do you want to play catch the bubble? We never ended up playing it the other day.'

'Can it be just us?' I asked. 'There's something else I want to do. You're so good at making things that I was hoping you could help me with something special.'

'Ooh,' said Oceana, intrigued. 'I'd love to!'

After school finished, Oceana and I swam over to her house which is near my dad's at the other side of Scallop City. She lives in a giant twisty seashell that has sea-glass windows. It's very pretty. We went up to her bedroom and Oceana got out all her craft things while her pet turtle,

Cleo, played nearby with Inkibelle. There was so much stuff! Beads, glitter, buttons, fabric, sequins, and shells. We could create anything we wanted!

'What exactly is it that you want to make?' asked Oceana.

'A headdress,' I replied. 'I think I need to make something that makes me feel more . . . like me!'

'That's a good idea!' Oceana said. 'How about something black, green, and glittery then? Maybe with an octopus on it like Inkibelle! A sequinned octopus!'

'An octopus!' I said, feeling excited.
Oceana always has the best ideas!

'It could have green crystals all over
its tentacles,' I added. 'To be like emeralds.
Like my name! And I could have some see-
through black fabric coming from my top

that will float about in the water. Ooh, and I could paint my nails black to match!'

'It would really suit you,' said Oceana.

I paused for a moment.

Would wearing an octopus on my head be a bit too . . . different? It would look nothing like my mum's headdress, or Delphina's or Auster's. It might make make me stand out even more and I was already worried about merpeople gawping at me. Surely I didn't want to give them *more* to gawp at.

'I suppose it doesn't sound very *princessy* though,' I said.

'I don't think we should worry about that. Let's just make something you love,' said Oceana.

I closed my eyes and imagined myself sitting with my family, wearing my octopus headdress. And it made me feel ... good!

Suddenly, I felt inspired and sparkly. And fizzy with excitement! I remembered what Auster said about how there was no point in pretending you're someone you're not.

'OK,' I said, glancing at the clock. 'We had better get started!'

★ ★ ★

I arrived back at the palace that evening feeling tired but excited. Under my arm I carried a large box with my new headdress inside.

'What's in the box?' asked Mum

when I came through the door.

'You'll see tomorrow!' I replied.

'Have you decided whether you're coming in the royal carriage tomorrow?' asked Auster.

'I have,' I said. 'And I've decided that I will!'

Mum beamed.

'But . . .' I continued, 'I'm going to be wearing something a bit different and I'd like you to trust me.'

'Trust you, eh?' said Auster, raising his eyebrows. Then he smiled, a big happy grin. 'That's wonderful news Emerald. We'll look forward to having you in the carriage with us tomorrow.'

Chapter FIVE

I woke up early on the day of the Ocean
Parade—there was so much to do! I got up
and had breakfast with my family and then
swished back up to my room to get ready.
I still felt nervous about going in the
carriage with everyone staring at me, but
now those feelings of nerves were mixed
with excitement too.

When I was ready, I swam downstairs to meet Mum, Auster, and Delphina. They were all floating by the great front doors of the palace waiting for me.

When I appeared, their mouths dropped open in amazement. I was wearing my new headdress—a dark green sequinned octopus that curled around my head with tentacle suckers made from emerald-like crystals. I had painted my nails black and dark starry fabric billowed and glittered all around me. Inkibelle floated nearby, a sequinned emerald-coloured bow on her head.

'Wow!' said Mum. 'You look . . .'

'Fabulous!' yelled Delphina. 'Spellbinding!'

'Erm . . . different,' said Auster, but his eyes were twinkling. 'I see you took my advice on board?'

I nodded.

'I was thinking about what you said and I realized that I would feel so much more confident sitting in the carriage if I felt more like myself. Even if it does make me stand out.'

'Well, I think you look perfectly, magically *you!*' Auster grinned.

'Yes,' agreed Mum, smiling. 'You're very talented to have made such a beautiful, intricate and *quirky* headdress.

How did you do it?'

'It was all thanks to Oceana!' I replied. 'And you all look amazing too!'

I meant it. Mum looked sparkling and regal in her pearly tiara. Auster looked impressive in his huge gold headdress and Delphina looked charming in all her princessy sparkle.

'Let's go!' said King Auster.

I felt the nerves squiggle around inside me again as Auster opened the great front doors of the palace and led us outside. the carriage was waiting—shimmering and shining in the rays of magical sea light. We all got in and I shuffled up next to the window with Inkibelle on my lap. Outside the palace gates I could see crowds of merpeople, waiting expectantly. I took a deep breath and my mum gave my hand a squeeze.

The dolphins set off and the carriage began to float towards the palace gates, heading out into Scallop City. Everywhere I looked there were merpeople dressed in their sparkling best. Beads, jewels, pearls, shells, and glitter twinkled back at me from every direction. I looked out for my friends and waved out of the window. It wasn't quite a royal wave like Auster's—it was my version instead! I smiled at the crowd and my smile felt real! I was so happy to be in the royal carriage with Mum, Auster, and Delphina. What's more,

I realized that *no one* was gawping. Not in the way I had imagined. I felt a bit silly for thinking that everyone would be so concerned with the way *I* looked. The crowd was a sparkling array of different outfits, styles, and fashions.

I loved it all!

The carriage glided through the water along the streets of Scallop City. Music was playing and merpeople were dancing. The atmosphere was electric! I couldn't help jiggling in my seat too, and Inkibelle began to bop her little tentacles about.

Suddenly, I spotted my friends. They were floating in a little group outside Eel's Emporium. Marina was wearing the beautiful outfit that Oceana had designed for her and Oceana looked enchanting, in a sheer turquoise cloak *covered* in sequin spangles. When they saw me they waved and waved! I waved back excitedly.

'Auster,' I said suddenly. 'Can we stop the carriage? Please?'

Auster hesitated for a moment, but then he nodded.

'I don't see why not,' he said. Auster stuck his head out of the window to call for the dolphins to stop swimming. I swished off my seat and opened the carriage door, swimming out. The merpeople around us gasped. I swam over to my friends and gave them a huge hug.

'Auster!' I shouted. 'Come and meet Oceana. She's the mermaid who made my headdress!'

I pushed Oceana to the front of the crowd. Auster swam out of the carriage, towards us. He looked impressed.

'It's a pleasure to meet you Oceana,' he said. 'Emerald's headdress is incredible!'

Oceana looked embarrassed but very pleased.

'Thank you,' she whispered. 'But it was nothing really . . .'

'It wasn't *nothing*,' said Auster. 'It was very kind of you to help your friend. I know it means a lot to Emerald.'

'It does,' I agreed, happily.

'Would you like to ride the rest of the way in the carriage with us?' asked Auster.

Oceana's eyes grew as big and round as jellyfish.

'Me?!' she squeaked.

'Yes!' I said, my heart exploding with happiness. There was only one thing better than riding in the royal carriage wearing my octopus headdress, and that was riding in the carriage wearing my octopus head dress with my friend by my side! I took Oceana's hand and dragged her towards the carriage. We wriggled in together and she sat down beside me on the seat, fidgeting.

Delphina was excited to have another mermaid in the carriage with us too, and we all sat there giggling and laughing while Auster and Mum shook the hands of all the merpeople in the crowd nearby. Then they both returned to the carriage and we set off again. I waved and waved, until my hand felt like it might drop off!

The carriage swept on through the parade until finally we reached the end of our journey back at the palace, where lots of fancy food stalls had been set up. We swam out of the carriage to enjoy the celebrations. Auster swished straight over to a food stall and handed a seafood skewer to each of us.

'Mmm!' said Delphina.

'It's nice,' said Oceana. But in my ear she whispered 'Not *quite* as nice as the coral floss and sea ices in the centre of Scallop City though!'

'True!' I agreed. 'But the thing is, I think we are supposed to stay in the palace grounds now that the parade is over.'

I felt a bit disappointed. It would be fun to find Marina, Finn, and Aqua.

'It *did* look fun down in the centre of Scallop City,' Delphina said. 'But we can have fun here too! I know all the best food stalls and look, there's some fish balloons!'

I looked over to where some beautiful balloons were bobbing in the water, all with rainbow shimmery scales.

'I'll get one for you!' said Delphina kindly. She whooshed over to the balloon stall just as Auster came swimming over with some delicious sweet seaberry smoothies. A moment later, Delphina swam back with a balloon trailing behind her, and handed it to me.

'Oh, that's pretty!' Oceana sighed as we both gazed at it for a moment. Then a band started to play and Oceana and I decided to have a dance, watching the way the balloon bobbed and glinted in the sea light. As we were twizzling, twirling and loop the looping I saw Delphina swim up to Mum and Auster and say something to them. A few minutes later they all came swimming over.

'Delphina says that the three of you would like to go into the centre of Scallop City?' Auster said.

'Oh um . . .' I began.

'I'd *really* like to go!' said Delphina, giving Mum and Auster her most charming smile. 'I saw they had coral floss and sea ices when we went past in the carriage!'

I held my breath, waiting to see what they would say.

'I'll tell you what,' Auster said. 'Why don't we *all* go!'

We climbed back into the carriage and the dolphins pulled us back through the streets of Scallop City, towards the

centre, where
Oceana and
I spotted our
friends. They were
taking it in turns to
balance on a manta rays,
using them to whizz through the water.
Finn was whooping with delight as
he swooshed up, down and all around,
holding tightly onto the reigns.

'Ooh!' said
Delphina. 'I'd
like a go on the
manta ray!'

'Me too!'
said Oceana.

'Me too!'
said Auster and
I turned to him
in surprise.

'I used to be very
good at manta ray gliding when I was a
young merboy,' he said. 'I'll have to show
you all!'

We swam out of the carriage and over
to my friends who seemed surprised to see
us.

'We didn't think you'd be back!' said
Aqua.

'I'm glad you made it though,'
grinned Marina. She had a crown of sea
flowers on her head and the petals waved

97

gently in the underwater current. I smiled back at her. My heart felt full.

We all watched Auster have a go on the manta ray, holding tightly onto the reigns and whizzing backwards and forwards.

'Oops!' he said, as he fell off it for the hundredth time. I think he might have been telling a fib about being good at it as a merboy! I saw Mum roll her eyes, fondly.

There was a crowd gathered around us now. Everyone was laughing

as they watched the king play around

on the manta ray and he looked like he

was having the best time ever.

I suddenly realized that, just like

me, Auster didn't always look or act

exactly like a royal either.

'That was fun!' Auster whooped when he finally finished manta ray gliding. 'Thank you for suggesting we come here Delphina and Emerald!' His headdress was wonky and his hair was all messed up, but he didn't seem to mind. 'What shall we do now?'

'Get coral floss and sea ices?' said Delphina hopefully.

'Your wish is my command!' replied Auster. 'But where do we get that from?'

'I'll show you!' offered Oceana.

We all followed her across the crowded square to a food stall and chose our flavour of coral floss and sea ice. I went for purple seaberry! Then we sat down to eat them. Inkibelle kept poking out her tentacle to steal little bits!

'Delicious!' said Auster, smacking his lips. 'Do you know, I have never had a sea ice before.'

'Really?!' said Mum in surprise. 'Maybe we ought to come out into Scallop City more often!'

'I'd love that,' said Auster. 'You and Emerald can show me all the best places to eat.'

I smiled. I couldn't help it. I felt like I was overflowing with happiness! It was so nice to just sit here, tail to tail with all my friends, Mum, Delphina, and Auster, listening to music, eating sea ices, laughing and feeling like *myself*. This year's parade was turning out to be just as good as last year's parade . . .

No, actually . . .

It was *better*!

Turn the page
for some
FIN-TASTIC
things to make
and do!

Quiz

Which merperson are you?
Take the quiz to find out!

1. You are going to the Ocean Parade! How would you like to take part?

A. I would be riding in the royal carriage, waving out of the window at my friends.

B. I would rather be watching the parade with all my friends and a big stick of coral floss.

C. I would be skating alongside the royal carriage on my manta ray!

2. What do you like to do in your spare time?

A. Drawing and making things at home.

B. Playing with my pets or spending time with animals.

C. Skateboarding in the park.

Results

Mostly As

You are a creative super star just like Oceana! You love using your imagination to create amazing pieces of art. You're a great friend who is kind and empathetic.

Mostly Bs

You are a natural around animals and your friends love spending time with you just like Emerald. You are fun, funny and kind.

Mostly Cs

You are bursting with energy and your enthusiasm is infectious just like Finn! You love playing with your friends and using all that energy to spread a bit of happiness everywhere you go.

C. Invite them to play a game of rounders with a group of friends, to cheer them up.

B. Ask if they were OK.
A problem shared is a problem halved.

A. Ask if they would like to hang out and do something I know they enjoy.

3. If a friend is in need, what would you do?

Fruit skewers

There's lots of yummy food at the Ocean Parade,
including Delphina's favourite, seafood skewers.
If seafood isn't your thing, here's how you
can make fruit skewers at home.

What you will need:

★ Some wooden kebab skewers

★ A knife

★ A grown up to help

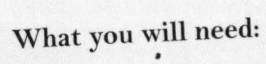

Method:

1. Cut and peel your fruit into tasty bite-sized morsels.

2. Push them on to the kebab stick in an order of your choice.

3. Enjoy!

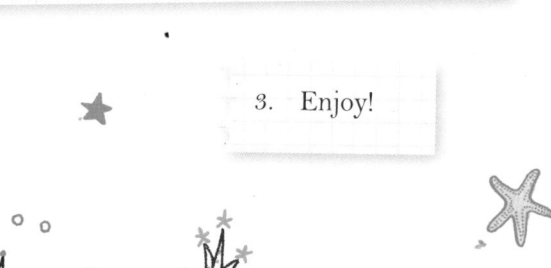

How to make your very own headdress

Emerald and Oceana made a fabulous headdress that was totally, uniquely perfect for Emerald. Why don't you think about all the things you love, and make a totally unique headdress of your own?

What you will need:

- Glitter paper
- Scissors
- Hole punch
- Ribbon
- Plastic gems, sequins, or anything else you can think of to decorate your headdress.
- PVA glue

Method:

1. Cut out a headband shape from the glitter paper.

2. Punch a hole in both ends of your headband shape.

3. Thread a ribbon through each hole and tie a knot in the end to secure it.

4. Decorate your tiara.

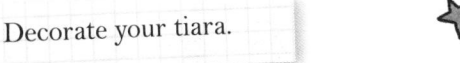

Mermaid cupcakes

These tasty cupcakes are perfect for any celebration.

Ingredients
For the cakes:

- ⭐ 100g caster sugar
- ⭐ 100g butter, softened
- ⭐ 100g self-raising flour
- ⭐ 2 eggs
- ⭐ 1 tsp vanilla extract
- ⭐ Food colouring in a colour of your choice (greens and blues are nice for anunderwater theme)

For the icing:

- ⭐ 200g butter, softened
- ⭐ 200g icing sugar
- ⭐ Sprinkles and other edible decorations of your choice!

Equipment:

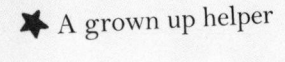

- Weighing scales
- Bowl
- Sieve
- Whisk
- Cupcake cases
- A 12-hole bun tin
- Piping bag
- A grown up helper

Method:

1. Preheat the oven to 180°C/Fan 160°C/gas 4.

2. Place cupcake cases into a 12-hole bun tin.

3. Mix sugar and butter together in the bowl, then sift in the flour.

4. Add the eggs and vanilla extract.

5. Add a couple of drops of food colouring. Remember, a little goes a long way!

6. Fill each paper case with the mixture.

7. Bake for 15-20 minutes or until the cakes are well risen and springy to the touch (ask an adult to help).

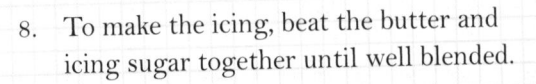

8. To make the icing, beat the butter and icing sugar together until well blended.

9. Stir in a few drops of food colouring (this can be a different colour to your cakes, or the same).

10. Put the icing mixture into an icing bag.

11. Once the cakes are completely cool, pipe icing onto each cake and decorate your sea-themed cupcakes with sprinkles.

12. Enjoy!

How to make your own sea ices

Emerald and her friends love sea ices.
They are the perfect way to cool down after a
busy afternoon manta ray gliding, and now
you can make your own version.

Ingredients:

- 150ml apple juice
- 150ml lemonade
- 150ml tropical fruit juice

Equipment:

- Ice lolly moulds and sticks
- Jug and a long spoon for mixing
- Measuring jug

Method:

1. Measure out your ingredients and pour them into a jug.

2. Give the mixture a good stir with a long spoon.

3. Pour the mixture carefully into the ice lolly moulds until they are almost full.

4. Put your ice lolly sticks into the top of the mould.

5. Carefully place in the freezer.

6. Wait for the lollies to freeze. This will be the hardest part because after all this hard work, you will really want a sea ice, but you must be patient!

7. When the lollies have frozen, take them out of their moulds, share with friends and family, and enjoy!

Party game

Emerald, Oceana, Finn, and Aqua love to play catch the bubble. It's a special merpeople game where you have to race each other through the water after a silvery, magic bubble.

This is a different game that you can play on land with your friends or family. If you want to really make a splash with this catching game, you can use a water balloon instead of a ball.

1. You all stand in a small circle and throw the water balloon to one another.

2. When the water balloon has been thrown to everyone in the circle, everyone takes a step backwards, so the circle is now bigger.

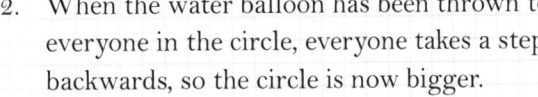

3. Carry on throwing the water balloon round the circle and each time everyone has thrown and caught, take another step back.

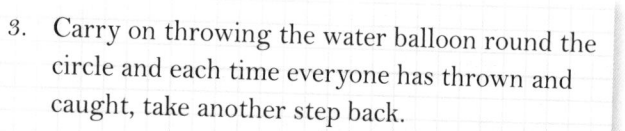

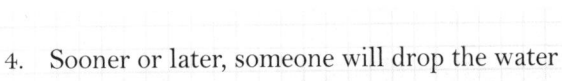

4. Sooner or later, someone will drop the water balloon and splat—they will get wet!

5. Make another water balloon and start all over again!

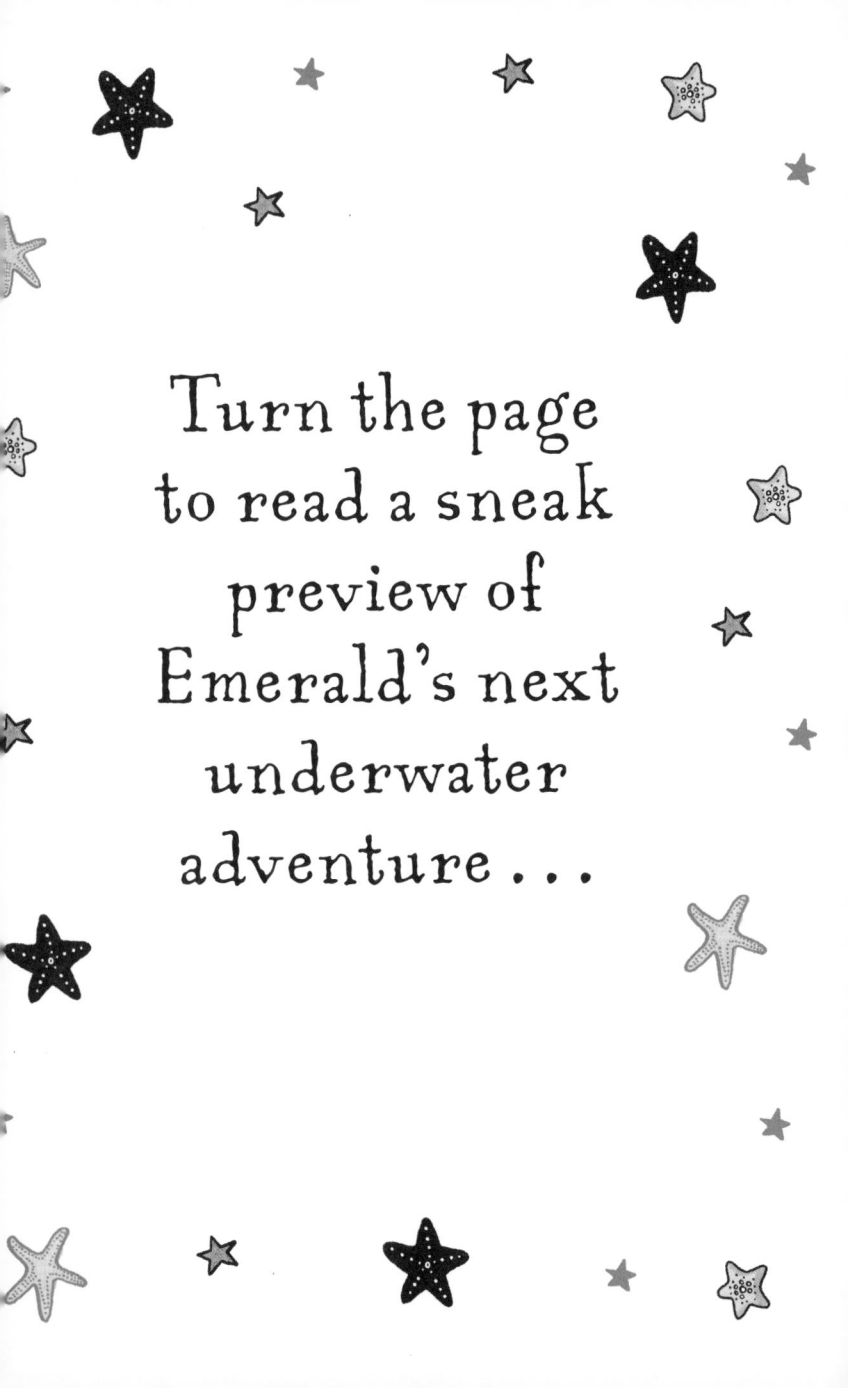

Turn the page
to read a sneak
preview of
Emerald's next
underwater
adventure . . .

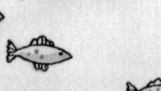
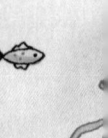

EMERALD

and the Sea Sprites

Chapter ONE

I was enjoying a lazy Saturday lying on my clamshell bed, propped up by sea-sponge pillows, and reading my new book, *Aqua Magic*. Dad had given it to me only the day before—it was about an explorer mermaid called Cleodora Blue who went off in search of sea sprites—tiny creatures who live far away in a magical

part of the ocean. They looked so cute in the illustrations with their little faces and delicate gills. I couldn't help stroking the pictures with my finger!

I turned the page, watching how the metallic illustrations shimmered in the underwater light. Then I took a sip of my seaberry smoothie which was sitting on my bedside table and nibbled a slice of mermaid toast, spread with deliciously sweet seaweed butter. I felt very content and peaceful. Palace life can be busy and I was still sort of getting used to it. My mum married King Auster recently (which makes me a princess—yes really!) but I only live here half the time. The other half

I spend with my dad who lives in our old house on the other side of Scallop City.

I turned the next page in my book. The tiny sea sprites twinkled up at me. I smiled and reached again for my drink.

'Emeraaald!' came a sudden, familiar voice from outside my bedroom door. It was so loud that it made me jump and I almost dropped my smoothie onto my little pet octopus, Inkibelle! Without knocking, my stepsister Delphina came bursting into my room, her royal curls bouncing as she swished over to where I was lying on my bed.

'Emerald!' she said. 'How are you? *I'm* well thank you. I was just feeling a little

bit bored. I thought you might like to play!
Do you want to play?'

'Erm . . .' I said.

Delphina began swimming around
my room, poking at everything on my
shelves, lifting the lid of my jewellery box
to peer inside, and running her fingers
across the spines of all my books. Then
her gaze settled on my doll's house.

'Ooh!' she exclaimed. 'Let's play with
your doll's house!'

'Erm,' I said again.

I wasn't sure that I liked the idea of
Delphina playing with my doll's house.
I've had it ever since I can remember and
it's very special! It's a shimmery blue-

green colour with turrets and swirly
pink shell-shaped spires. There's lots
of furniture inside, which I've collected
over the years (I usually get a new piece
for every birthday and sometimes I save
up my pocket money to buy something
myself). There are chairs made from
twisty coral, a bathroom sink fashioned
from an upturned clamshell, a tiny sea
urchin footstool and lots of teeny crystal
perfume bottles.

'Oh, come on Emerald,' begged
Delphina. 'Let's play!'

She opened the front of the doll's
house and sat back to gaze inside.

'Can *I* at least play with it?' she asked.

'Pleeease? You can stay there and read your book if you *must*.'

'*I guess so,*' I said reluctantly. Delphina seemed so enthusiastic that I didn't want to feel mean by saying she couldn't play with it.

I took a sip of seaberry smoothie and tried to read my book but it was hard to concentrate with Delphina in my room. I kept hearing her rearranging the furniture in my doll's house. My tail started to twitch with annoyance. Eventually I jumped off the bed in a flurry of bubbles and swam down to join Delphina, putting the sea sprite book on the floor. If I was going to let my stepsister play with my special doll's house, then I wanted to make sure she played with it properly!

'The clamshell bed goes in the bedroom,' I explained, taking it out of the tiny attic room where Delphina had placed it and putting it back where it was supposed to be.

'Oh, OK,' said Delphina, but she wasn't really listening. She had picked up a tiny harp and was now running her finger along the strings so that they made a faint tinkling sound. Without meaning to, I shot my hand out and snatched the harp, cradling it to my chest. I could just imagine those delicate strings going *snap, snap, snap!*

Delphina looked surprised for a moment but then her attention was diverted by a miniature pirate's treasure chest, full of tiny, sparkling jewels and gold coins.

'Oooh,' she breathed, opening the lid and poking her finger inside so that the jewels and coins overspilled, floating down onto the floor.

I gritted my teeth. Playing doll's house with Delphina was starting to feel quite stressful. One by one I began to pick up the little gold coins while Delphina looked around for the next thing to investigate. Her gaze rested on my book.

'Sea sprites?' she asked. 'I've heard of

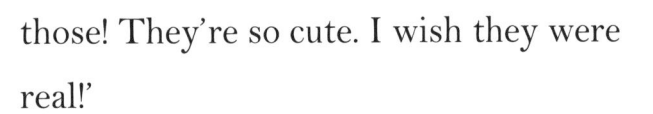

those! They're so cute. I wish they were real!'

Delphina grabbed the book and began to leaf through the pages.

I frowned.

'What do you mean, you wish they were real?' I asked. 'Of course they're real! This book is all about an explorer mermaid called Cleodora Blue who goes on a mission to find some! They're very wild creatures you know. They live in a magical part of the ocean which is hard to find, in a special coral reef.'

'Really?' said Delphina. 'I thought they were just . . . *made up*!' Her mouth hung open like a gulper eel.

I laughed.

'They're definitely real,' I said. 'They're just rare.'

I took the book from Delphina and began to riffle through the pages.

'Look,' I said, pointing at a photograph of Cleodora Blue holding one of the sea sprites in her hand. 'They're very friendly apparently.'

'They're teeny!' said Delphina. 'I like their little gills and their smiley faces!'

'Me too,' I agreed. 'I'd love to see one in real life!'

Delphina stared at me for a moment and her eyes went very big and round and thoughtful. Then suddenly, she grabbed

onto my arms.

'We *could* see one in real life Emerald!'
she said excitedly. 'If we went on our *own*
explorer mission! Why don't we sneak
out of the palace and go and find some sea
sprites ourselves! Oh come on, let's do it!
I'm so *bored* today!'

I stared at my stepsister in surprise.
Delphina is usually the *perfect mermaid
princess.* She would never normally suggest
breaking the rules!

'You?!' I said. '*Sneak* out of the
palace?'

Delphina blushed.

'Well Dad would never agree to us
swimming away from Scallop City,' she

said, 'would he?'

'Definitely not,' I replied.

'So we'll *have* to be a bit sneaky,' said Delphina. 'I just think it will be worth it to see a real sea sprite! Don't you agree?'

'I suppose,' I said, trying to sound as though I wasn't that bothered, although inside my heart was beginning to pitter patter and my fins tingled with excitement.

'So that's settled then,' said Delphina. 'We're going on a sea sprite mission! Find your binoculars and bring your book—I saw a map in there and it looks like we need to go north. I'll go and get us a bag of snacks. Meet you in the palace gardens

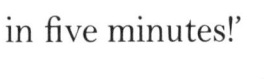

in five minutes!'

Then in a whirl of glittering bubbles Delphina swished round and swam out of my bedroom. I watched her go before grabbing Inkibelle to my chest and hugging her excitedly.

'We're going on an adventure!' I said.

Harriet Muncaster, that's me! I'm the
author and illustrator of Isadora Moon,
Mirabelle and Emerald books. Yes really!
I love anything teeny tiny, anything
starry, and everything glittery.

ISADORA MOON
Goes to School

Half vampire, half fairy, totally unique!
Harriet Muncaster

ISADORA MOON
Goes Camping

Half vampire, half fairy, totally unique!
Harriet Muncaster

ISADORA MOON
Has a Birthday

Half vampire, half fairy, totally unique!
Harriet Muncaster

ISADORA MOON
Goes to the Ballet

Half vampire, half fairy, totally unique!
Harriet Muncaster

ISADORA MOON

Makes Winter Magic

Half vampire, half fairy, totally unique!

Harriet Muncaster

ISADORA MOON

Goes to the Fair

Half vampire, half fairy, totally unique!

Harriet Muncaster

ISADORA MOON

Goes on a School Trip

Half vampire, half fairy, totally unique!

Harriet Muncaster

ISADORA MOON

Gets in Trouble

Half vampire, half fairy, totally unique!

Harriet Muncaster

ISADORA MOON

Has a Sleepover

Half vampire, half fairy, totally unique!
Harriet Muncaster

ISADORA MOON

Puts on a Show

Half vampire, half fairy, totally unique!
Harriet Muncaster

ISADORA MOON

Goes on Holiday

Half vampire, half fairy, totally unique!
Harriet Muncaster

ISADORA MOON

Goes to a Wedding

Half vampire, half fairy, totally unique!
Harriet Muncaster

ISADORA MOON

Meets the Tooth Fairy

Half vampire, half fairy, totally unique!

Harriet Muncaster

ISADORA MOON

and the Shooting Star

Half vampire, half fairy, totally unique!

Harriet Muncaster

ISADORA MOON

Under the Sea

Half vampire, half fairy, totally unique!

Harriet Muncaster

ISADORA MOON

Gets the Magic Pox

Half vampire, half fairy, totally unique!

Harriet Muncaster

ISADORA MOON

and the New Girl

Half vampire, half fairy, totally unique!

Harriet Muncaster

MIRABELLE

From the world of ISADORA MOON
MIRABELLE
Gets up to Mischief

Half witch, half fairy, totally naughty!
Harriet Muncaster

From the world of ISADORA MOON
MIRABELLE
and the Naughty Bat Kittens

Half witch, half fairy, totally naughty!
Harriet Muncaster

From the world of ISADORA MOON
MIRABELLE
Has a Bad Day

Half witch, half fairy, totally naughty!
Harriet Muncaster

From the world of ISADORA MOON

MIRABELLE
Breaks the Rules

Half witch, half fairy, totally naughty!

Harriet Muncaster

From the world of ISADORA MOON

MIRABELLE
in Double Trouble

Half witch, half fairy, totally naughty!

Harriet Muncaster

From the world of ISADORA MOON

MIRABELLE
Takes Charge

Half witch, half fairy, totally naughty!

Harriet Muncaster

From the world of ISADORA MOON

MIRABELLE
and the Magical Mayhem

Half witch, half fairy, totally naughty!

Harriet Muncaster

To visit
Harriet Muncaster's
website, visit
harrietmuncaster.co.uk